big & SMALL

Original Korean text by Hui-jeong Yun
Illustrations by Gong-joo Yun
Korean edition © Dawoolim

This English edition published by big & SMALL in 2017
by arrangement with Aram Publishing
English text edited by Joy Cowley
English edition © big & SMALL 2017

Distributed in the United States and Canada by
Lerner Publishing Group, Inc.
241 First Avenue North
Minneapolis, MN 55401 U.S.A.
www.lernerbooks.com

ISBN: 978-1-925234-87-9
Printed in Korea

Welcome to the Seashore

Written by Hui-jeong Yun
Illustrated by Gong-joo Yun
Edited by Joy Cowley

This is the seashore.
What life can you see?
Just look under the water.

6

The sea is full of living things.

This is a jellyfish.
It swims by folding its body
in and out, in and out.

This is a mudskipper.
See its bulging eyes?

This is an American lobster.
It crushes prey with a big claw.

This is kelp seaweed.
Small fish hide in it,
safe from predators.

The sea urchin
protects itself
with sharp needles

A sea urchin moves with its tube feet.

Go deeper!

This is an octopus.
It has eight legs.
Or are they arms?
"Octo" means eight.

11

The tide comes in and then
goes out twice a day.
Now the tide is going out.
See the bare mudflat?

Where are all the creatures?
They are hiding under the muddy surface.

13

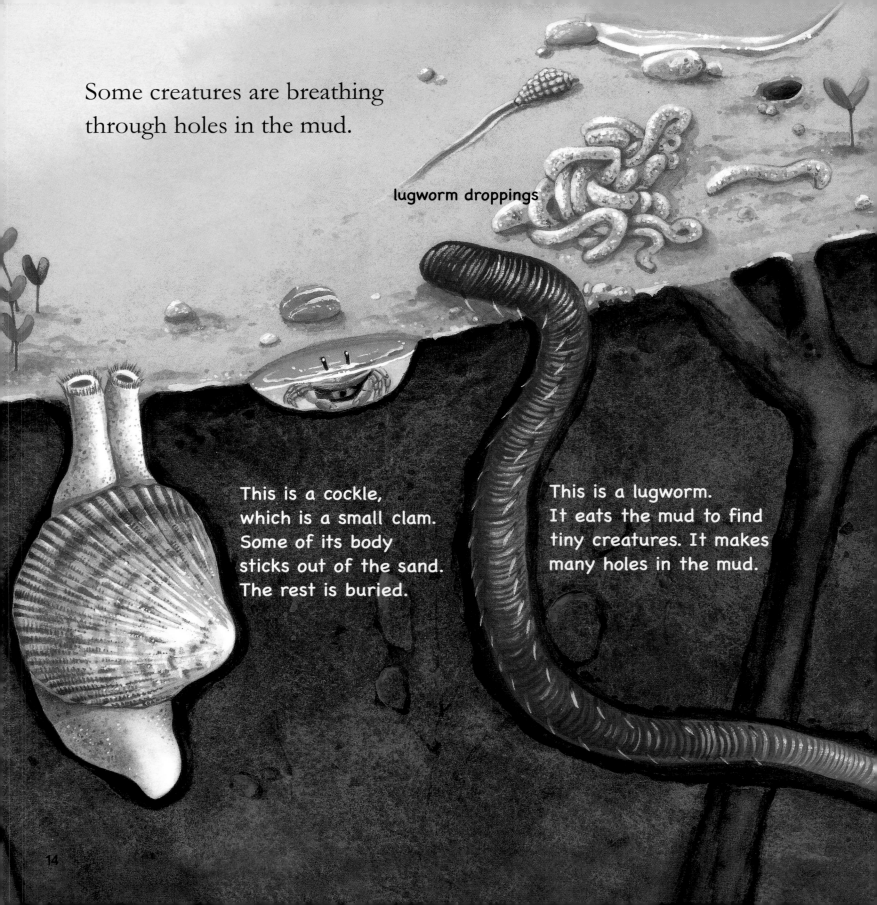

Some creatures are breathing through holes in the mud.

lugworm droppings

This is a cockle, which is a small clam. Some of its body sticks out of the sand. The rest is buried.

This is a lugworm. It eats the mud to find tiny creatures. It makes many holes in the mud.

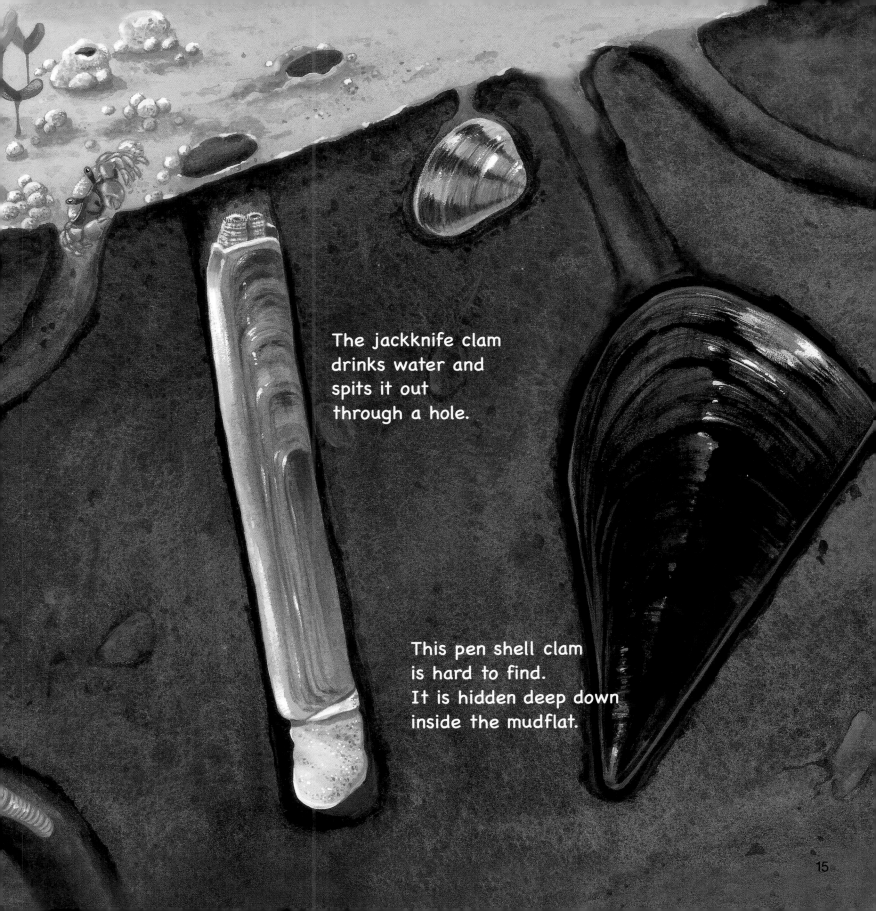

The jackknife clam
drinks water and
spits it out
through a hole.

This pen shell clam
is hard to find.
It is hidden deep down
inside the mudflat.

A sand bubbler crab
spits out bubbles of sand.

The hairy-legged crab
stacks up balls of sand
to make a den.

16

An empty conch shell
is a house for a hermit crab.

These little crabs are always
busy on the sandy beach.

This is a Japanese ghost crab
under the sand.
Only its eyes peek out.

Gastropods include snails and slugs. They feed on dead fish and clams on the mudflat. These creatures slide on their bodies to move.

There is always plenty to eat on the mudflat.

This is a moon snail.
It drills a hole
in a clam's shell.
Then it eats the clam.

A mudskipper wanders
across the mudflat to feed
on shrimp or young crabs.

These are mussels
attached to rocks.

Barnacles are also
attached to rocks.
They make a strong glue
that keeps them in place.

At the end of the mudflat
are some rocks. Many sea
creatures live on these rocks.

Some creatures, like these oysters,
look like the rock they live on.

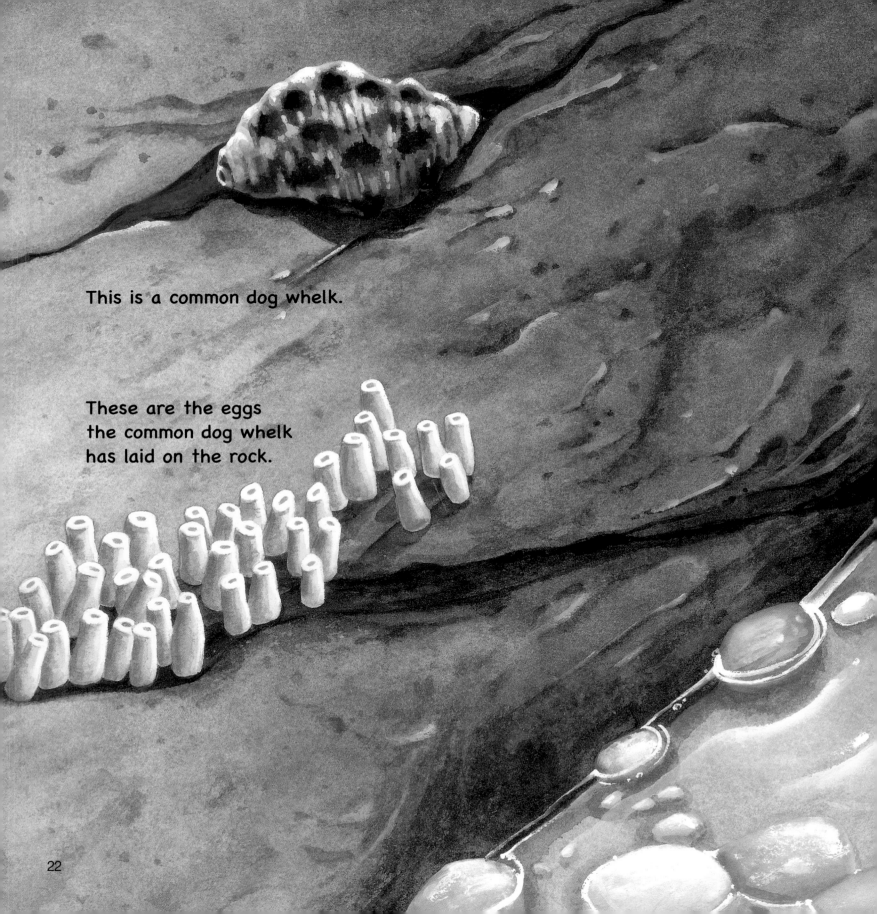

This is a common dog whelk.

These are the eggs
the common dog whelk
has laid on the rock.

What are these creatures?

These creatures are
sea lice. They eat
dead crabs and fish.

23

Here is a small pool between some rocks.
It was left behind after the tide went out.
What lives here?

Oysters

Starfish

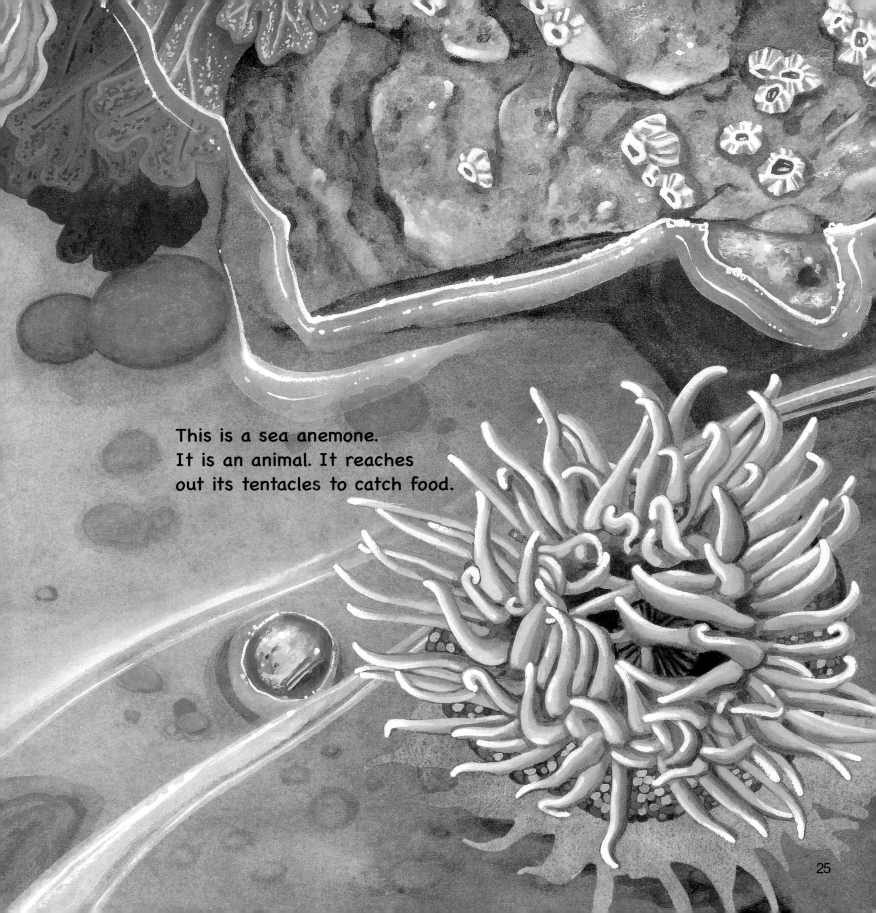

This is a sea anemone.
It is an animal. It reaches
out its tentacles to catch food.

Many birds also live
on the seashore.
They search the mudflat
for small creatures to eat.

This egret looks for food
before the tide comes in.

This snipe has a long bill
that it pokes into the mud.

This hungry bird is
a Mongolian plover.

Splash! Splash!
The tide is coming in,
covering the mudflat.
But six hours later,
it will go out again.

Welcome to the Seashore

Many different plants and animals live on the seashore. They live above the sand, under the water, in tidal pools, and buried in the mud. Discover how plants and animals work together and survive in their seashore homes.

Let's think!

How does a jellyfish swim?

What protects a sea urchin?

What does a lugworm make in the mud?

How do gastropods move?

Let's do!

Discover different kinds of shells from the seashore. Look at a starfish, a conch shell, a mussel, and other kinds of shells from the book. Do the shells feel rough or smooth? Are they thin or thick? How are the shells alike? How is each one different? See the different kinds of shells that sea creatures make and live inside.